A MAN
OF HER
CHOICE

What if you stopped searching …
and created him instead?

AMEEN AMANULLAH S

 Scribe

A Man of Her Choice

Publisher: Inkscribe Publishing Pvt. Ltd.

ISBN Number: 978-1-969259-25-8

Contents

Acknowledgement

To,

Dr. D. Faritha Banu, B.S.M.S., B.G.L.

Additional Collector

District Revenue Officer

There are people who inspire.

There are people who guide.

And then, there are those rare souls who do both—quietly, generously, without ever seeking recognition.

You didn't just believe in me.

You stood beside me when no one else saw what I was trying to build.

You supported me not just with words but with action.

With unwavering presence.

With selfless help—even financially—when creation felt too heavy to carry alone.

This book would not have reached these pages without you.

You are stitched into its heart, woven into every line.

And I will never forget what that means.

Thank you—not just for supporting my creative field... but for becoming a silent part of my courage.

With respect, pride, and endless gratitude,

— **Ameen Amanullah S**

Preface

To the woman reading this:

This story is not about fantasy. It is not a tale of fate or luck.

It is a journey of creation—from desire to design, from silence to connection.

If you're a woman, you may find yourself here. Not in the details, but in the essence.

In the clarity. The ache. The knowing. The becoming.

If you're a man, this may feel like a mirror—sharp and quiet—reflecting what it means to be chosen not by chance, but by intention.

This is not about perfection.

This is about the moment a woman stops searching for what completes her—and chooses to build it instead.

Turn the page, and let this story unfold through you.

Chapter 1

All Mine but One

The air always smells like possibilities at sunrise.

Soft linen curtains, fresh-ground espresso, and sandalwood oil still lingering on my skin from last night's bath. It's a ritual now—the morning stillness before the world knocks on my door.

My name? Doesn't matter. You already know me.

Or, at some point, you will.

I'm twenty-two. I run a boutique studio—fashion, styling, curation, and quiet power stitched into every thread we sell. I'm not someone who talks too much about ambition. I just live it. Quietly. Sharply. Every single day.

People see me and say I've got it all. And maybe, I do.

A brand that's growing faster than I can count. A team that trusts me.

A bank account that doesn't flinch.

Clients who whisper my name in rooms I've never entered. Skin that still smells like youth.

A brain sharper than my heels.

I don't wake up to prove myself. I wake up already convinced.

But in that beautiful, silent stretch of each morning... between the first sip of coffee and the first buzz of my phone, there's a question that visits me like a ghost.

Not "what's next." I always know what's next. But:

Why does it still feel like something's...unfinished?

I've asked myself this too many times. Maybe I just think too much.

Maybe not.

When you live a life so carefully built — every brick placed with intention—it's hard not to notice the missing tile in the mosaic.

And for me, that missing tile has always been *him*.

Not *a man*. Not *any man*. But *him*.

The one who fits.

I've dated. Oh, I've dated.

They've come with their slick charm and late-night texts, their ambition, and their flattery. I've met the ones with poetic eyes and corporate titles. I've met the ones who dance with danger, who drive too fast, and who kiss like they've got something to prove.

But each time, it ends the same way.

A tilt. A scratch. A sliver of misalignment. One's too afraid of my intensity.

Another wants me to tone it down.

One says I'm perfect but still flirts with shadows.

Another says he's all-in but folds the moment life gets complex.

It's not that they're bad. They're just... **not it**.

You know that feeling? When the shoe almost fits—but bites at your heel? You walk in it anyway, convincing yourself you'll break it in.

You don't. You blister.

I'm not looking for a prince or a saviour.

I'm not seeking validation or fairy-tale kisses. What I want is simple—in theory.

A person who fits the rhythm of my mind. Who understands silence without fearing it.

Someone who meets my eyes and *gets it*—without needing a monologue.

And no, I'm not expecting perfection.

But I am done compromising on alignment.

Let's be honest—the world doesn't teach women to think this way. We're told to be grateful, to be soft, to adjust.

I don't adjust. I *choose*.

That's the thing most people miss about women like me. We're not arrogant. We're not picky.

We're just...clear.

And that clarity? It comes at a cost. Loneliness.

Restless nights.

That ache in your chest when you've done everything *right*, and yet, something still doesn't click.

It's not that I'm sad. I'm just *aware*. So yes—I have it all.

Except for one thing. And this story?

It's about what happens when a woman like me decides to stop searching for that missing tile…

and instead, *builds it*.

Chapter 2

The Empire She Built

And this story?

It's about what happens when a woman like me decides to stop searching for that missing tile…

and instead, builds it.

But before you understand *why*, you need to understand *me*. Not the surface. Not the headlines.

But the engine beneath the elegance.

See, it's easy to dismiss a woman like me. Pretty. Poised. Successful.

They think it was luck. Or a man. Or a trend. But I didn't land here by chance.

I *designed* this life. From ash. From the edge. From exactness.

I was twenty when I started with nothing but an idea— that fashion wasn't about fabric. It was about *identity*.

Who you are when you're not performing. Who you become when the fit feels *right*.

I found a forgotten space above an old bookshop, where the ceiling leaked in winter and the walls still whispered stories of tenants long gone. That space didn't intimidate me. It inspired me.

I scrubbed it myself. Painted it myself. Curated every corner with obsessive love.

And I didn't wait for the world to discover me. I *made it look*.

One client. Then another. Then ten.

Not because I advertised, but because I *listened*. I asked what they hated about shopping. About clothing. About themselves.

And I didn't just sell them beauty. I gave them *permission*.

To own their shape. To stop hiding. To walk differently.

I remember staying up nights, redesigning silhouettes, and blending cuts that weren't in books. My fingers bled sometimes from testing stitching machines I couldn't afford to replace. I handwrote thank-you notes for every order. Learnt scent psychology to pair fragrances with personalities.

I even designed a digital mirror that adapts lighting and fits in real-time—before tech people told me it was possible.

They laughed when I pitched it. Now they want to license it.

I say that not with pride. But with a record.

If I wanted something, I created it.

If I imagined it, I found a way to bring it into form. My

mind?

It doesn't daydream. It *delivers*.

The boutique grew. Quietly. Elegantly. No press. No noise. Just the right people

— finding their way to the place where they were finally seen.

And I—I didn't just sell garments. I studied people.

Watched how they stood when they wore the right jacket. How their voice changed with the right neckline.

I learnt everything. About posture, about persuasion, about presence. Because I wasn't just building a brand.

I was learning what it meant to *craft a being*.

And that's why…

When I say I'm ready to build the man of my choice—I mean it.

I've built harder things. With less.

In a world that never handed me blueprints, I've drawn my own. And this next creation?

It won't be a garment. It won't be a perfume. It won't be a moment.

It will be a **man**.

But let me tell you a truth I don't say out loud. Not in interviews.

Not in rooftop conversations.

Not even in the silence of my own home. I want to be

valued.

Not for what I've built. Not for how I look.

Not for the way I walk into a room and rearrange its energy without trying.

I want someone who sees the woman *beneath the precision*. The girl who stayed up at night doubting herself.

The woman who keeps her voice calm when her heart is tired.

The soul that's carried everything—quietly, gracefully—without once asking to be held.

I want someone who doesn't compete with my strength—but *adores* it. Who doesn't flinch at my power but *protects* it.

No, I don't want to be rescued. God, no.

But yes…

I want to be **pampered**.

Not with gifts. With attention. With softness.

With that steady, wordless kind of care that says,

"You don't always have to be the strong one. Not with me."

I've never pleaded for that. Never chased it.

But in the deepest part of me—the part no one touches—it *waits*. It watches.

It wonders if such a person could ever exist. And maybe that's why I stopped searching.

Because I didn't want a man who *tried* to be that. I wanted a man who *was* that.

Naturally. Instinctively. Wholly.

A man who could look at me and *just know*—not what I wear,

not what I earn, but what I *need*.

And what if that man didn't exist?

Then, like everything else in my life… I'd create him.

Chapter 3

The 100% Illusion

People assume a woman like me gets approached by the perfect man all the time.

They're not wrong.

I get invited to high-end dinners, curated retreats, and industry panels—always with a line of admirers who say the right things and smile the right way.

They come in suits, sometimes in silence. Some lead empires.

Some fake one.

But if you ask me what most of them have in common? They admire me.

But they don't **see** me.

They're in love with the image.

The packaging. The precision. The myth.

And when they peel back the surface, they realise I don't need saving. And for some reason, that frightens them.

So they fall into categories:

The ones who try to tame me.

The ones who try to compete with me.

The ones who think their money makes us equals. The ones who stare too long but listen too little.

I learnt how to recognise the tilt in a voice. The tiny ego bruises when I outthink them.

The way they fumble with praise, unsure if I'm the prize or the threat.

I met artists who were insecure. CEOs who were shallow.

Healers who needed more healing than they offered.

Men who claimed they wanted someone like me—until they had to stand beside me.

I stopped expecting. Started observing.

Smiled politely, and let them go before they could disappoint me too loudly. But then…

He arrived.

Not through a dating app. Not through friends.

It was at an investor's gala, somewhere between the second glass of wine and a debate on sustainable fashion.

He didn't come in loud. He came in *aligned*.

He asked the right questions.

Not surface. Not invasive. Just…precise. He listened—really listened.

Spoke with intention. Not just charm.

We spent two hours standing near a sculpture no one noticed. And in that time, I started to wonder—*could this be it?*

He didn't flinch at my ambition.

He quoted obscure thinkers I actually admired.

He looked at me like he'd already *understood* me—not from research, but resonance.

And for the first time in years, my guard—the one built with steel and stitched with logic—*softened.*

We met again. And again. In quiet corners.

In pages of shared poetry.

In laughter that came unforced.

He didn't ask what my net worth was. He didn't try to prove anything.

He just... *fit.*

Until, of course, he didn't.

It started with a small thing—a story that didn't quite match.

Then a conversation where he slipped, mentioning something I had never told him.

I checked. Quietly. Thoroughly.

Turns out—he wasn't just lucky. He was *informed.*

He had studied me.

Not out of admiration—out of calculation.

Background checks confirmed it:

He wasn't who he said he was. The credentials were forged.

The career? Inflated. The charm? Scripted.

He had crafted himself to mirror my desires—just enough to get inside. To get close.

To get access.

And maybe—eventually—to get control. Of me.

Of my business.

Of everything I'd built.

I didn't scream.

Didn't cry.

Didn't even confront him.

I simply… watched him burn the bridge without knowing it was already collapsing beneath him.

And then I walked away. Quiet. Clean. Unshaken.

Not because I wasn't hurt.

But because I had seen this too many times. And now? I was *done* hoping.

He was the final proof.

That the man of my choice doesn't exist. Unless I **create** him.

Chapter 4

The Blueprint

You'd think heartbreak looks like tears.

Like mascara-stained pillows or half-drunk wine glasses. Mine didn't.

It looked like silence. And spreadsheets.

And seventy-two hours of uninterrupted studio time—no calls, no meetings, just me and my empire humming back to life.

It looked like fabric swatches laid out like a meditation ritual. Sandalwood is burning slowly in the corner.

Emails answered with precision. Orders finalised with calm authority.

Pain, for me, never drips out dramatically. It *redirects*.

Into systems. Into strategy. Into art.

That man?

He didn't ruin me.

He reminded me.

Of who I am.

Of how far I've come.

Of how many times I've walked through flames and emerged not burnt—but

sculpted.

The betrayal stung. But it didn't scar.

Because it never touched the part of me that mattered.

He didn't break my heart.

He tried to trespass in my mind. And he failed.

A week later, I was back in full command of the studio. Orders were flowing.

The Milan showroom was confirming expansion.

A collaboration with a scent designer in Paris was back on track.

My team noticed it too. That quiet fire in my walk.

The rhythm in my commands. The old me—but sharper.

I wasn't smiling more. I was *breathing* deeper.

Something had shifted.

That part of me that kept hoping, just a little, that someone would find me—understand me, hold me—had gone quiet.

Not bitter. Not sad. Just... at rest.

The world had shown me enough.

And I had finally, finally stopped waiting. That's when the idea came.

Not like lightning. Not like madness.

But like breath.

Slow. Certain. Solid.

I was standing in the fabric vault that day.

Shelves towering over me, filled with silks, organzas, and hand-dyed cottons I'd collected from every corner of the globe. Each roll is labelled, catalogued, and protected.

Every one of them—a story I had chosen. A texture I had shaped.

And then, out of nowhere:

What if the man I want was never meant to be found?

The question didn't rattle me. It calmed me.

Because it wasn't a sign of giving up. It was the beginning of **taking charge**.

What if he wasn't out there—waiting—already made? What if he was meant to be **built**?

Not through fantasy.

Not some artificial puppet. Not in arrogance or control.

But in *intention*. In care. In clarity.

I've designed entire systems of identity.

I've watched women transform in my studio—from self-doubt to radiance—with a single outfit, a shift in stance, or a well-placed collar.

I've learnt how power is held and how it's passed. How presence is shaped from posture.

How voices change with confidence.

How belief is sewn into the seams of what you wear.

So tell me:

If I could shape all that… Why not shape **him**?

Why not start at the very beginning?

Not with a man full of baggage, ego, or layers shaped by someone else's narrative.

But a blank page.

No control issues. No fragile pride.

No inherited views of how women should be.

A boy.

Raised with kindness, respect, and emotional depth.

Trained not to worship me—but to *walk beside me*. Taught to admire strength, not feel threatened by it. To recognise beauty without trying to own it.

A boy who would, one day, become a man… And that man would meet me—not as a saviour. But as an *equal echo*.

It sounded wild. Unconventional.

Maybe even unhinged to someone else. But to me?

It felt like the most grounded idea I'd ever had.

I wouldn't interfere in his growing years. Wouldn't play mother.

Wouldn't watch him grow—because I didn't want to feel *maternal*. This wasn't about parenthood.

It was about *partnership*.

I would fund everything.

His birth, his school, his books, his home.

I'd shape the blueprint—and let life raise him with care and grace.

Until he was twenty-one. And I… would be forty-one.

Exactly two decades of preparation.

Two lifetimes moving toward one meeting.

Not as creator and creation. But as **choice meeting choice**.

He wouldn't know me.

But he would know himself.

And maybe—just maybe—he would recognise me without ever being told.

That night, I opened my journal. No to-do lists.

No business goals.

Just a title at the top of the page:

"The Man of My Choice"

And below it, I began to write… Not traits.

Not measurements.

But *essence*. Energy.

Presence.

What I wanted to feel when he entered the room. How I

wanted to *breathe* around him.

Not what he would say—but how he would *see* me.

And as I wrote, the fear dissolved. The ache quieted.

And all that remained… was certainty.

Chapter 5

A New Contract

Ideas are powerful.

But execution is where I live.

Once the thought took root—that I could build the man of my choice—it didn't remain a fantasy for long.

I didn't hesitate. I didn't journal about it for months. I began **planning**.

Not out of desperation. Out of direction.

I knew what I wanted, and more importantly, I knew how to move toward it with elegance.

This wasn't going to be a child born out of longing. It would be a life shaped with purpose.

I wasn't chasing motherhood. I was designing *alignment*.

The first step was quiet. Discreet. Private.

I met with a reproductive rights consultant—a woman I trusted. She worked with high-profile, high-boundary clients. Her name never appeared in glossy interviews. She knew how to read intent, not just paperwork.

I told her what I wanted. Not in vague terms.

A surrogate.

Anonymous sperm, selected with sharp filters—not just for genetics, but for presence.

A legally protected distance.

The child raised by someone else—with my financial backing, but without my presence.

"I don't want to raise him," I said.

Her eyebrows lifted—not in judgement, but in curiosity.

"I want him raised *well*. With love, with structure, with education. But not by me. I don't want the bond of a mother. I want the clarity of a creator."

She paused. Then nodded.

"You don't want to *love* him like a mother," she said softly. "You want to *meet*

him like a woman." Exactly.

The arrangements began.

She connected me to a woman—not young, but not old—someone strong, emotionally sound, and fully consenting. A mother already. She had raised two boys. She understood what it meant to let go.

When we met, she wasn't intimidated by me. She looked me in the eye.

Listened carefully. Asked real questions.

And I respected her for that. I laid it all out on the table.

"I want to fund everything," I told her.

"Your health, your comfort, your future. But there's one

rule—I don't want contact after the birth. I don't want photos. I don't want to know how he grows. I will pay for it all, but I won't witness it."

Her brow furrowed. "Why?" she asked.

I answered calmly. "Because I don't want to feel like a mother. I want to meet him someday not through memory—but through *presence*. Like two adults. Like destiny."

She didn't answer right away. She sat still for a long minute. Then she nodded.

"I can do that," she said.

The contract was written carefully.

The compensation was generous—more than generous.

There were additional trusts, educational funds, stipends, and security arrangements.

The child—*my design*—would be raised privately but with everything he needed.

He would read. He would think.

He would learn kindness and boundaries and the art of stillness.

He would be taught how to handle silence—how to look people in the eye without fear.

His body would be cared for. His mind would be nurtured. But not spoilt. Never spoilt.

And one day...

When he turned twenty-one… We would meet.

I wouldn't tell him the whole truth—not right away. I would let the world unfold between us.

Not forced. But inevitable.

As the paperwork was signed, I didn't feel nervous. I felt *awake*.

As if a part of my future had just moved one inch closer.

Was it bold? Yes. Unorthodox? Absolutely. Controversial? Maybe.

But I wasn't doing this to please the world. I was doing this to **complete my world**.

Not a child. Not a project.

A man.

The man of *my* choice.

Chapter 6

A Boy Designed

The child was born on a Tuesday. I did not attend the birth. There was no need. The process had already been activated, the conditions already established.

By the time I received confirmation, the legal, medical, and contractual structures were already in place. The surrogate had followed protocol. The guardianship was transferred per terms. No disruption. No sentiment.

I did not ask for a photograph. I did not want to know his weight, the colour of his eyes, or the way he cried. None of that was relevant.

This wasn't about a baby. This was about execution. A project with a twenty-one-year timeline.

The instruction file was thirty-two pages. It covered five verticals:

1. **Cognitive Conditioning:** Beginning at twelve months, the child would be introduced to pattern-based learning. No screens. No overstimulation. Daily exposure to analogue tools: puzzles, blocks, and neutral colour palettes. No character branding. No television. A library of hand-selected literature organised by

developmental stage.

2. **Physical Development:** Motor skills before sports. Core strength before flexibility. Formal movement training beginning at age six. Martial arts (non-violent discipline-based form only) introduced at nine. Postural reinforcement sessions twice monthly. No sugar-based diet. Monitored hydration. Structured rest. No devices permitted in sleep zones.

3. **Emotional Regulation:** At age four, implementation of behavioural journaling. The guardian was to document incidents of frustration, resistance, curiosity, and boundary testing. Therapy was not introduced unless escalation occurred. Emotional coaching was preferred—Socratic method, calm response, and consequence-based logic.

4. **Exposure Protocol:** No exposure to social media, commercial television, or celebrity culture until at least seventeen. Music was to be instrumental. Philosophy introduced before romance. The guardian was instructed to prioritise environments that emphasised stillness, silence, and resilience.

5. **Mentorship:** Three male figures were identified in advance. Each from different spheres—art, science, and philosophy. All emotionally intelligent. All hand-vetted. Their role: to model consistency, not charisma. Presence, not

performance. Scheduled interactions began at age twelve.

There was a delivery cadence. A format. A system. But none of it involved me.

I did not review progress metrics. I did not track performance. I did not allow deviation from design to affect my state of mind.

Because deviation was not a variable. The design was binary: either it succeeds, or it doesn't. And I had already removed myself from the middle.

It was not my place to interfere. It was not my role to reassess. I had appointed the best. And in that delegation, I found peace. No birthdays. No gifts. No letters. No deviation.

He was not mine. He was an outcome. A response to inefficiency in the existing system of compatibility.

There was no specific expectation. No checklist of traits. I never wrote down what he should become. That was intentional. Because expectation narrows. Projection distorts.

This was about alignment—not fantasy. Character—not charm. Clarity—not control.

Every reader might imagine something different. That is as it should be.

What he would become, I left undefined—not because I lacked direction, but because I believed in emergence. I believed that when presence is designed with integrity, it arrives without needing labels.

I never watched his journey. I never measured his outcome.

Because it was never about *watching him form*. It was about *meeting him formed*.

Meanwhile, I expanded.

My design houses multiplied. A studio in Lisbon. A textiles lab in Kyoto. A collaboration with an architect in Dubai that merged form and fragrance into a retail experience.

I spoke at conferences. I declined awards. I dated only when it was convenient.

Most men didn't get past the second meeting. Those who did rarely returned after the fourth. I never invited the same person twice in one season.

And I never explained myself.

Because what explanation would suffice? What words could articulate the fact that I was already moving toward something—someone—engineered over decades?

So I lived. I built. I refined. Not with love. With precision.

He wasn't growing up to please me. He was growing into a presence that might one day mirror mine.

That was all.

But until then, I would not interfere. That was the point. Control does not mean closeness. It means distance by design.

And when he was ready—twenty-one years old—we would meet. Not as mother and son. Not as origin and outcome. But as two trajectories… finally intersecting.

Chapter 7

Disappearing Act

The system was running. Quietly. Cleanly. Twenty-one years to go.

I didn't linger on it. There was nothing to monitor. Nothing to adjust. I had done my part.

And so I disappeared—not from the world, but from that part of the narrative. I returned fully to the rhythm I had built. The empire. The vision. The solitude.

I travelled more. Worked deeper. Ate slower. Expanded with clarity. My calendar was full, but my mind stayed quiet.

And yes, I dated.

Not because I was searching. But because I was alive.

The men came in many forms. Some elegant. Some clumsy. Some are fascinating in the first hour and forgettable by the third.

They approached me at art openings, on flights, in boardrooms, and in cafes. Most had confidence. A few had charm. Fewer still had pause—that rare quality of knowing how to stay still in a world obsessed with noise.

I never dated out of boredom. I dated with the same

curiosity I brought to a new scent profile or a rare textile: something to be explored, experienced, and understood.

Some were younger. Drawn to the structure, I carried it like a scent. Some were older. Drawn to the mystery I never tried to explain.

But they all came in with assumptions. And I watched them quietly unpack them.

One believed power was a mask for loneliness. One tried to teach me how to relax—as if joy were something I hadn't tasted more fully than most. One adored my strength… until he realised it wasn't a phase.

Another said, "You intimidate me." I didn't flinch. I only smiled. Because what he meant was, *I don't know what to do with a woman who doesn't need me to define her.*

Some wanted to impress me with influence. Others tried to disarm me with vulnerability. Some tried to build fantasies around me—their idea of a strong woman, softened by their presence.

But I didn't correct them. I didn't console them.

 Simply let them reveal themselves. And when the moment came—the moment I knew nothing further would evolve—I ended it gently.

No drama. No punishment. No mess. Just a quiet close.

Not because they weren't good men. But because they weren't the one I was preparing to meet.

I never said that out loud. But I knew.

Each interaction taught me something. Not about men.

About *myself*. My calibration. My clarity. My patience.

I never used love as a distraction. Never used bodies to numb. When I wanted touch, I chose it. When I wanted silence, I stayed in it.

I had learnt how to say no before curiosity turned into inconvenience. I had learnt that intimacy didn't require narrative. It just required presence—and timing.

Every experience was filtered through the knowledge that my story wasn't ending in romance. It was culminating in alignment.

And alignment doesn't beg to be chased. It arrives.

So while the world tried to guess who I was waiting for, I gave nothing away. Because this wasn't about the world. It was about a meeting that hadn't happened yet.

And when it did—everything I'd withheld, everything I'd refined, everything I'd designed—would be ready.

Not for validation. For recognition.

But until then, I lived. And let go. Again and again. Without resentment. Without regret. Just space.

Held for the one I had built it for.

I treated my body the way I treated my business—with intention.

Not out of vanity. But because discipline is a form of clarity. I didn't punish it with diets or flood it with routines just to feel control. I maintained it like a vessel that was holding something precise—presence.

My meals were clean. Balanced. Designed to support sharpness. I wasn't chasing a shape. I was maintaining energy. I ate the way I dressed—

minimalist, but rich in depth.

Fasting wasn't a trend. It was a method for stillness. I avoided foods that dulled me. Sugar. Excess salt. Anything that left a fog. Because my mind wasn't just a tool—it was my signature.

And the body needed to keep up.

Exercise was daily. Quiet. Non-negotiable. I didn't run. I moved. Pilates. Barre. Long, silent walks. Nothing loud. Nothing punishing. Just enough to keep the body aligned with the pace of my mind.

I considered strength training briefly. But I chose refinement over resistance. Not because I feared weight. But because I understood precision.

The body ages. Yes. But it can age *on purpose*.

I didn't need to stay young. I needed to stay *undiluted*.

Because when I finally stood in front of the one I had prepared to meet—I didn't want to explain who I had been.

I wanted to *embody* it.

Without apology. Without need. Just...readiness.

So I trained not for appearance. I trained for presence.

And I lived in that presence every day until the moment arrived.

Chapter 8

Living Loud, Loving Lightly

I've always known how to command a room. But I never needed to command a heart.

In the years after the boy was born—my designed creation—I returned fully to myself. To my empire. To my rhythm. And in that rhythm, I carved space for something else: freedom. Not loneliness. Not absence. Just freedom.

This phase of my life never felt like waiting. It felt like breathing again. Like silk after steel. Like the second sip of wine, once your tongue stops bracing for the bite. I didn't long for love. I wasn't hollowed by craving. I simply recentred—and in that centre, I explored.

I dated when I wanted to. Not for validation. Not to mend anything. Just because I could. Just because it delighted me.

Sometimes it was the younger ones—bright-eyed, impulsive, curious. Drawn to my gravity like moths to a controlled flame. They brought laughter. Adventure. Youthful chaos that ended by Sunday.

Other times, it was equals. Men who led their own spaces. Who had their own charm. Who could order wine with confidence and read my eyes. But none of them matched my interior.

They'd flirt. I'd smile. There were weekends—Paris, Mumbai, Istanbul. Cafés with hidden rooftops. Hotel rooms with velvet curtains and gold-threaded silence. Kisses with no promises. Mornings with soft exits.

And then I was back—to myself.

My mornings still began with sandalwood and espresso. My studios still expanded. My voice still echoed in boardrooms. My reflection still met my gaze in the mirror; I never sought approval.

"I am not lonely," I've reminded myself more than once. "I am alone by design."

There was no bitterness. No ache. Only fullness.

I never hid my relationships. I just never caged them. They were seasons. Songs. Chapters. Not epilogues.

"There is no shame in enjoying moments that do not last forever."

I've seen others chase validation through marriage, monogamy, and titles. I don't judge them. I just chose differently. Not because I feared love—but because I refused to settle for its diluted version.

"Let it be full, or let it be nothing."

People speculated. The world admired. Men whispered about the ones who 'almost' had me. But I remained unbothered.

Because I was never waiting. I was becoming.

And in that becoming, I gave myself permission to live every shade of womanhood—without apology. Without pause.

I didn't need companionship to feel whole. But when it came—briefly, lightly—I welcomed it like rain after heat.

Every man I shared space with left a moment, not a mark. And that was enough.

I wasn't saving myself for anyone. But I knew something no one else did:

One day, the man of my choice would arrive. Not through luck. Not through longing. But through the life I had already placed in motion.

Until then? I lived loudly. Loved lightly. And never forgot who I was building myself to meet.

Chapter 9

Empire in Motion, Currents in Silence

By now, my brand wasn't just a boutique. It was a movement.

Three flagship studios—each in a city that mirrored a part of me: the elegance of Milan, the pulse of Mumbai, and the fire of São Paulo. An immersive scent exhibition in Marrakesh—where visitors didn't just smell perfumes, but experienced scent-memories bound to colour, mood, and memory. Collaborations with glass artists in Prague, textile historians in Kyoto, and behavioural psychologists in Zurich.

Every decision came from instinct. Every product had a soul.

I no longer "ran" the company—I orchestrated its energy. My employees stayed longer than the industry norm. Suppliers called me by name, even from other continents. Journalists didn't describe me as a businesswoman—they called me a force.

My days were full—curated, intentional. But never rushed.

In the mornings, I mentored young designers. They sat

beside me in a sunlit corner of the studio, sketching—not beneath me, but with me. In the afternoons, I drew in silence. No meetings. No noise. Just fabric, light, pencil, and presence. Evenings were for dining with clients who'd become confidants. The conversations weren't always business. Often, they were about identity, loss, reinvention.

"Business is not about numbers," I told my board. "It's about stories. And we are in the business of shaping identity—one silhouette at a time."

I had become a symbol. But even symbols can carry solitude.

Behind the lighting tests, the panels, the PR dinners—there was still a question, whispered only within:

"Is there anyone who knows the version of me that doesn't lead? Doesn't win? Just breathes?"

I didn't dwell on it. I didn't ache for answers.

I simply folded that question neatly into the drawer of things life may answer one day—or may not.

Because I wasn't just building a brand. I was building a life so complete, so textured, that if someone ever entered it, they'd have to meet me exactly where I stood.

I wasn't waiting like a damsel. I was preparing like a queen.

And the boy—the life I initiated so long ago—no longer threaded through my daily rhythm. He wasn't a hope. Or a regret. Or even a memory I lingered in.

He was simply… paused. Filed. Archived with intention. A design I had placed in motion, then set aside.

I didn't light candles on his birthdays. I didn't wonder how he looked. I didn't follow his growth like a mother might.

Because this was never about motherhood. It was about precision.

I gave the world my design—and then I moved forward.

I built. I expanded. I travelled. I created systems of elegance and impact. I spoke on stages. I whispered truths in closed-door mentor sessions. I flirted. I disappeared. I returned.

And never once did I feel like something was missing.

Until one morning. When an envelope arrived. Unmarked, except for the words:

"He's ready."

That's when I remembered—I had written a chapter that was now about to begin reading itself aloud.

And everything—everything I had forgotten I prepared for—was about to walk into my life.

Not like fate. Not like fantasy.

But like something long ago designed and finally… delivered.

Chapter 10

The Arrival

Finally, the day had arrived. His twenty-first birthday.

For him, it was just another milestone. But for me—it was everything. Not an ending. A beginning.

He was now the age I had waited for. The age I had chosen, calculated, and invested two decades into reaching. The moment wasn't marked with banners or champagne. It was marked with silence. With precision. A dinner invite. Nothing more.

I extended it through a formal channel—a professional gesture. An opportunity. An offer to intern, to observe the studio, to meet a woman who had heard about his progress and wanted to offer him a role.

He accepted.

No surprise. The offer was curated well—positioned, polished, and intriguing. And then… he arrived.

He walked in just past seven. No entourage. No noise. Just presence.

A tall frame. Shoulders held with grace, not arrogance. A body shaped not by vanity, but by discipline. His walk was fluid and unhurried—the way people move when they are not chasing anything.

The room didn't pause for him. *I* did.

He wore a deep grey shirt, tucked into quiet black trousers. No logos. No posturing. Just control. Clean. Intentional.

And his face... He was beautiful—not in the fragile, fleeting way that fades with youth. But in the structural, self-aware way that draws people without effort.

His eyes scanned the room. Then landed on me. He didn't know. Of course, he didn't know.

To him, I was just the founder of the company. A powerful woman. A distant figure. A new chapter in his young career.

But I? I was looking at the culmination of everything I had shaped without touching.

He walked over. Extended his hand. Introduced himself. His voice was calm. Balanced. Neither rehearsed nor intimidated.

We sat. We talked.

I asked about his education, his interests, and his principles. Not as a test. But as confirmation.

He answered with clarity. With the kind of simplicity that only comes from depth. He didn't try to impress. He just... existed well.

He asked questions too. Not flattery in disguise. Genuine curiosity. He wanted to know how I built what I built. How I chose certain partnerships. Why I

rejected a key investor three years ago. Yes, he knew.

He'd done his homework.

I asked about the books he read. The ones he re-read. I asked what kept him up at night—he said, "Ideas I haven't solved yet."

We discussed rhythm. Not just in music—but in people. At work. In silence.

I watched him sip water before speaking. I watched him listen without interrupting.

Every small gesture carried intention. It wasn't performance. It was present.

He spoke about his mentors. Not to name-drop. But to credit those who helped him calibrate his thinking.

There was a moment—maybe ten seconds—when he paused. Looked directly at me. Not with confusion. Not with expectation. Just with something that felt like recognition.

But he said nothing. And I didn't offer anything. Not yet.

We moved to dinner.

A quiet table by tall glass doors. Ocean in the distance. No music. Just light, curated dishes served by a staff trained not to interrupt energy.

He ate with the same presence he spoke with. Thoughtfully. With awareness. He didn't try to fill the silence. He let it breathe.

And I... I allowed myself to feel what I hadn't in decades:

The sensation of meeting someone for the first time,

knowing you had met him long ago.

Not in person. But on purpose.

I had waited years—silently, methodically—for this moment. And now, across this table, in a quiet villa set for two, he was here.

Not a boy. A man.

And not just any man. The man I had built space for. Without ever building him directly.

He didn't know that. But I did.

And in that moment, as he spoke about his thoughts on creativity, resilience, and self-work—I didn't need to analyse. I didn't need to ask for more.

Because I already knew: it was worth the wait.

Chapter 11

The Moment

I was mesmerised.

Not by his looks alone—though he was, objectively, stunning. It was his presence. Grounded. Gentle. Intact.

I had crafted the conditions. Built the blueprint. Delegated the shaping. But the outcome? That was beyond me.

And now, he sat across the table, breathing the same air, carrying the same poise I had carried my entire life.

It hit me without drama. Without music.

I got the man of my choice.

And yet, the moment that thought formed, another one followed: Now… I want him to feel I am the woman of his choice.

I shifted. Subtle. From professional to personal.

"So," I said, casually placing my glass down, "what's your idea of a partner? What matters to you in love?"

He blinked. Caught off guard. Then smirked.

"Whattt? That's getting off topic. This is supposed to be a professional meeting," he said, half-laughing.

I smiled—not flustered, not apologetic. Just...strategic. He was right. And also, *exactly like me.*

Clear boundaries. Intentional focus. The moment things veer into the personal without context, we raise a flag.

I saw myself in that response. My tone. My instinct.

He is my mirror.

And so, I pivoted. Gracefully.

"Oh, that?" I chuckled lightly, leaning back. "That's just my way of reading people. I ask odd questions sometimes. Helps me understand how someone thinks, not just how they work."

He nodded slowly. Accepted it. His body relaxed again.

"Hmm... that's fair," he said. "You do carry that interview-by-instinct vibe."

We both laughed. The moment passed. But I had learnt something:

To reach him, I'd have to speak the way I listen to myself—measured, intentional, never too soon.

And then he surprised me.

"I was meaning to ask," he said, his tone shifting slightly. "How did you manage this empire... alone? All these years? It's kind of extraordinary."

There it was. A door. One I didn't have to knock on—he opened it. And I stepped through.

"Honestly?" I said, softening my voice just a touch. "I stopped thinking of it as managing anything. I designed it. Then I maintained the design."

He leaned in, interested.

"Wasn't there ever a time when you thought... maybe share the weight?" I met his gaze.

"There were times people *offered* to share it. But most didn't understand the weight they were volunteering for."

He nodded slowly. Thoughtfully.

"So you waited," he said, more to himself than to me. "I designed," I corrected.

He smiled. And that smile—it wasn't flirtatious. It was knowing.

And from that moment forward, the space between us was no longer just professional.

It was a possibility.

I kept speaking. Answering his questions. Telling him about the early days, the expansion, and the struggles no one saw. The conversations I'd had with CEOs twice my age. The decisions I made while the world was watching... and the ones I made when no one was.

He listened—to every word. But then something shifted. I caught it. The way his eyes lingered a little longer. The way his brows tightened just slightly.

And suddenly I became aware—painfully aware—of myself. I was glorifying. Not sharing.

I had moved from presence into performance. And I knew it.

The real me—the part that usually stays hidden behind control—had leaked out. I had said too much. I was showing him the mountain without offering a path.

And for a brief second, I thought: *If I were him... I might reject myself.*

So I paused. Took a breath. And smiled.

"Would you like to take a walk?" I asked. He raised an eyebrow, surprised.

"This time," I added, "just personal. No business talk. I promise it'll be worth it."

He smiled back. "Sure."

I stood. Slowly. Calmly. And we left the table.

I didn't need to impress him. I needed to meet him. And that required space—not structure.

Chapter 12

The Walk

The streets were quiet, just as I'd hoped. A breeze, not too cold. The kind of evening that softens edges.

We walked side by side. No hand-holding. No awkward pauses. Just silence that felt full, not empty.

I glanced at him out of the corner of my eye. The man of my choice, walking next to me. He didn't know. But I did.

And something about that made me feel...light. Not giddy. Not nervous. Just present.

I had never felt like this walking next to a man. Not once. I had always led. Always assessed. Always observed.

But now? I found myself looking for small ways to impress. Not perform. Impress.

I did things—subtle, thoughtful—not loud. The kind of things that leave a trace without leaving a question.

And he noticed.

He didn't compliment me in the usual sense. He didn't flatter. He just... smiled. Paused. And said something simple.

But it wasn't what he said. It was how he said it. Like joy had slipped into his voice without permission.

That moment—that tiny, unfiltered expression—was enough.

Because I knew I had reached him. Not deeply. Not permanently. But enough to matter.

And in that moment, the woman who had rejected so many men, the woman who had said "no" more times than she could count, the woman who was called intimidating, unreachable, untouchable—

She had tried. For him.

She had chosen to put in effort. And she enjoyed it. The walk wasn't long. But it meant everything.

We talked. Lightly. Honestly. Nothing forced. Nothing impressive.

I let him speak more than I usually allow. I listened in a way I rarely do.

I wanted to know him. Not just the surface.

I wanted to know what made him slow down. What made him turn toward things instead of away?

At one point, he asked again, half-smiling, "Why the sudden walk? We were mid-discussion."

I returned the smile, this time slower. "Because sometimes, continuing a professional conversation in a different setting gives you more insight than sitting across a table ever could. This is still part of the interview, just not on paper."

He nodded. It made sense to him. That was the point.

I had to justify the shift—not for him. For us. Because he was right earlier. It began as a professional invitation. And he was watching for consistency.

So I delivered it. Not as a diversion, but as a strategy. And it worked. He spoke freely after that. And I let myself soften into the space.

I found myself reading his reactions, his steps, and his silences. And I began to respond—not with performance, but with presence.

The way I stood. The stories I chose to tell. Even the way I laughed—a little less restrained than usual.

Everything I did came from instinct. Not to manipulate. But to meet him there. And when we reached the end of the walk, I knew. He had enjoyed it too.

There was no rush to leave. No false politeness. Just that quiet tension of two people who don't want the moment to end.

But it had to.

So, I offered him the internship. Directly. No delays. No assistants. I told him I wanted him at the head office.

He nodded, surprised but composed. "Thank you," he said. "Truly."

I smiled. "You earned it."

We didn't hug. We didn't linger. Just one last look. And then I watched him walk away.

That night, I returned home. No wine. No work. Just stillness.

I replayed the walk in my mind. His words. His presence.

And for the first time in years, I didn't sleep. Not from stress. But from something else.

From wanting. From thinking. From remembering how he looked under the streetlight when he smiled.

I turned in bed. Reached for nothing. Just air. And the realisation settled:

This wasn't design anymore. This was love. Not imagined. Not abstract. But starting.

I found myself picking out clothes for the morning. Soft fabrics. Intentional lines. Not for the boardroom. For him.

My character didn't change. It softened.

Not because I was falling. But because I was finally meeting something I had created space for all along.

And now...I couldn't wait for morning.

Chapter 13

The Morning After

Morning came too slowly.

The night had been restless. I had turned more times than I usually allowed myself. My pillow still carried the trace of sandalwood from last night's bath, but it wasn't soothing—it was sharp, alert.

I had already picked out three outfits in my mind before sunrise. Laid them on the lounge chair. Soft shades. Clean silhouettes. Not boardroom bold—but subtly persuasive.

By seven, I was dressed. Hair done. Lips—soft nude. Earrings—none. Fit check? Passed. Fragrance? Just a trace.

But then, as I stood in front of the full-length mirror, something shifted. I looked at myself. Not with admiration. With critique.

"Really?" I whispered. "This excited?"

I was smiling without control. I was fussing with details. I—the woman who led mergers and launched boutiques across continents—was adjusting a cuff for a man?

That's when I stepped back. Mentally.

"Get back," I told myself. "Return to who you are."

The empire builder. The strategist. The woman who didn't tilt her world for admiration.

I took one last glance, gathered my bag, and left the house.

The car ride was usual. Playlist minimal. Phone on mute. My mind slowly shifting back to command mode.

As I entered the office, everything returned to rhythm. The elevator ride. The greetings. The tempo.

"Good morning, ma'am," said my PA, walking beside me as always. She handed me the day's brief.

"Your first meeting is in 30 minutes, the Paris call has been rescheduled, and legal sent back the contract drafts—"

I was nodding, responding as we walked.

So deep in discussion that I didn't notice him.

Not until I'd passed him entirely.

He was standing in the lobby. Waiting. Wearing that same calm posture, holding a folder, watching me walk by.

He'd said, "Good morning, ma'am." But I hadn't heard it.

Or maybe I had—just not consciously.

Because the moment I stepped into my room, it hit me like a bolt.

Oh, no. He's here.

The very man I had stayed up thinking about… the man

I had waited to see—I had completely forgotten in the flow of command.

"Call the new intern in," I told my PA. She blinked. "Yes, ma'am."

She turned. Then paused. "Is there anything specific you want him for?" I shook my head. "Just send him in."

She gave a small nod—a hint of curiosity in her eyes. He entered with a gentle knock.

I had just adjusted my hair. Checked my lips. I didn't know why. It was automatic.

He opened the door. "Hi, ma'am," he said, with that clear, steady tone. And I… I smiled. Too wide, maybe.

I wanted to say, "Don't call me ma'am." But I didn't.

Because I was his boss. Still.

"Did you have breakfast?" I asked. He nodded. "Yes. Thank you."

I ran him through the role. The responsibilities. The structure. I hired a team lead to guide him—someone capable, smart, and unobtrusive.

Everything was said with calm professionalism. No tremor. No tilt.

When we finished, I smiled politely. "All the very best. We'll be seeing each other around, professionally."

He stood. "Looking forward to it." Then he left.

I sat for a second. Let the moment settle.

I had handled that well. Didn't reveal anything. Didn't fumble.

But the moment he exited, I walked to my desk. Tapped the CCTV monitor. There he was. At his desk. Opening his laptop. Focused.

And then—it started.

The subtle looks. Female staff passing by more slowly. The receptionist adjusted her hair after glancing at him. A design assistant pretending to drop her pen.

I laughed. Softly.

So this is what possessive feels like. It wasn't jealousy. It was awareness. The kind that says:

"That one? That one's mine." But not yet.

Not officially.

And not until he feels it too.

Chapter 14

Field visit, Unscripted bond

There's something I do occasionally. I don't schedule it. I don't announce it.

I pick one employee—someone new, untested, or simply quiet—and take them along for a field visit. No preamble. Just a tap on the shoulder and a simple, "Come with me."

It's not a test they know they're taking. But it always reveals something.

Their attention to detail. Their patience. Their ability to function outside structure.

So that morning, as I stepped into the lobby, I spotted him. Sharp. Present. Reading something on his tablet.

I paused. Took one breath. Then said casually, "You. With me. Field visit."

He stood, no questions. A few of the others glanced over. One of the assistants whispered just loud enough for him to hear,

"She does this. Just observe and be sharp." He gave a small nod. And followed.

In the car, silence settled first. Then rhythm. He asked nothing. I offered nothing. But the atmosphere wasn't cold. Just be calm.

Two hours later, we arrived at the vendor showcase. A countryside design studio

— minimal architecture, glass walls, tall trees, soft air that smelt of cedar and ink.

He moved like he belonged. Took notes. Asked questions when needed. Never too much. Never performative. He spent ten minutes discussing weaving.

techniques with a fabric artisan, asking about climate impact on dye quality—with the kind of interest that wasn't rehearsed.

I watched from a corner as he interacted with one of the textile curators. He didn't try to impress. He absorbed. Responded. Disarmed the room with his calm.

Then I moved to my part—reconnecting with an old collaborator who greeted me with a warm, knowing nod. The team was stuck between two opposing aesthetic themes—earth tones clashing with jewel hues. I stepped in, offered a colour sequence that bridged both visions, and restructured the board with fluid hand gestures and quiet certainty. Within minutes, the confusion turned into cohesion. Even the junior stylists paused, nodding quietly, scribbling down my suggestions like notes from a masterclass. She had been stuck between two themes—I fused them in under a minute. Even the junior stylists took notes.

As we transitioned between booths, I caught him observing quietly—not just what I did, but *how* I did it.

Later, as we crossed paths again, he looked at me with a half-smile. "So this is how you've handled it all these years."

It wasn't a question. It was a compliment.

And I blushed. Not visibly. But enough that I turned toward the driver and said, "Take us to a café before we head back."

He didn't react. Just nodded.

We sat near the window. The café was quaint—quiet music, real coffee, and no work talk.

"What do you do when you're not building empires?" he asked. "Try not to rebuild them in my head," I said, smiling.

He laughed. It wasn't polite. It was real.

We talked about nothing urgent: how cities smell after rain. Why some people can't sit through silence. Whether espresso should ever be sweetened.

No roles. No agendas.

Just two people, sitting across from each other, pretending—just for a moment

— that none of the hierarchy existed.

Then, casually, he leaned back and asked, "Why didn't you ever marry? Any specific reason?"

I looked at him. Caught off guard. For once, I didn't have a response ready.

He saw the surprise and raised his hands slightly in mock

surrender. "I mean, it's post 6 p.m. You're not my boss now. I'm not your intern. Just two people sharing coffee, right?"

I smiled, shook my head slowly, and let out a breath. "Yeah... you're right."

I sipped my coffee, then leaned back. "So, coming back to your question... I've never seen a man who fulfils my expectations."

He tilted his head, intrigued. "Ohhh? Not a single one?" "Yeah..." I said softly.

There was a pause—the quiet kind, not awkward. And then he asked, almost playfully, "What's your type, then?"

I gave a soft laugh and returned the question, "Why don't you answer that first?"

He smiled and leaned in a bit, voice low and calm. "Someone who doesn't apologise for her clarity. Who knows when to lead and when to listen. Someone who moves with intent, not noise."

As he spoke, I saw it—not just the words, but the way he saw me in them.

And I felt it. A pulse of quiet happiness. Not because he complimented me. But because I saw myself in what he described.

Like he had described me—without knowing. And in that moment, something softened inside. It wasn't ego. It wasn't validation. It was something far rarer— recognition. After years of speaking into silence, here was someone reflecting back what I had always protected.

A part of me lifted. Like the wait had purpose. Like he was getting closer—step by step.

We didn't rush to leave. The conversation kept moving. From books to random memories. Two strange things we both notice that others miss.

And slowly... the evening dimmed. The light faded across the café windows.

The night had ended, but something had begun. As we stepped outside, he held the door—not out of chivalry, but timing. Our eyes met once, briefly. And that glance held more weight than any of the conversations we'd left behind in the café. I didn't look back as I stepped into the car—but I smiled the whole way home.

Something I couldn't name. But something I wouldn't deny.

Chapter 15

The Rhythm Between

The field visit didn't change anything on paper.

There were no decisions made, no contracts signed, no lines crossed.

But something shifted that day — not in what was said, but in everything left unsaid.

After we returned, we resumed our roles. I walked back into my office with the same posture, the same control, the same version of me everyone expected.

He did too. Focused. Discreet. Calm.

We passed each other in the hallway the next morning. A nod. Nothing more. A moment that anyone else would overlook.

But I felt it. The silence between us had changed its temperature.

We didn't speak about it. We didn't message that night. But I caught myself waiting for something—an update, an accidental text, a reason to engage. When none came, I respected it.

And yet, I also missed it.

A few days later, we left the building at the same time.

Coincidence. That's what I told myself.

I didn't say anything. Neither did he. But we walked toward the parking lot together, quietly, our steps adjusting to match.

It happened again the next day.

Then, an evening coffee. Not planned. Not deliberate. Just two people who didn't want to go home yet.

The conversation stayed light—books, art, people-watching. He asked questions that weren't probing, but they made me pause. I found myself laughing. Once, I even lost track of time. I hadn't done that in years.

That night, as I removed my earrings in front of the mirror, I saw something new in my eyes. A softness. Not weakness. Not infatuation. Just... ease.

What surprised me more was how much I didn't want to control it.

I had spent my life designing outcomes. Controlling environments. Managing perception. But with him, nothing was defined.

It wasn't romantic.

It wasn't professional.

It wasn't friendship either.

And that was the most dangerous part. It didn't have a name.

We began sharing rides sometimes—usually to an event or vendor meet. We never planned it, but we'd find ourselves standing near each other in the lobby, just as the car arrived. Neither of us questioned it.

Other times, a message would arrive on my screen—work-related, yes—but always with a small detail that didn't belong in a formal exchange. A line about the weather. A quirky headline. A smiley once.

I should've shut it down.

I didn't.

Because nothing he did was inappropriate. Nothing crossed a line. If anything, he was more respectful than anyone I'd worked with in years.

But I felt myself leaning toward him anyway.

Not with urgency. Not with risk.

With rhythm.

We never declared anything. We never even acknowledged it. But we began to exist in this unspoken orbit — two people moving side by side, with an understanding that something was happening between us.

I started to notice more.

The way he ran his fingers through his hair when he was thinking. The way he gave space in a conversation, never rushing to finish my thoughts. The way he looked at me—not with awe, not with ambition—but with clarity.

It unnerved me, how easy it was.

And it terrified me, how much I wanted it to continue.

I'd seen men crumble under less scrutiny. But he didn't flinch. That steadiness made me respect him even more.

When his internship ended, I didn't consult HR or loop in anyone from the leadership team.

I called him in myself.

The offer I made was not born from emotion. It was the result of observation. Of trust earned. Of the quiet certainty that he was meant to be here longer.

He didn't smile when I offered the role.

He didn't act surprised.

He just nodded — like he had already accepted it within himself.

"I've earned this," his body language said. "I know."

And I loved that.

I returned to my seat after he left the room. For a long time, I stared at the floor, letting the moment stretch.

There was no decision to make anymore.

I had already made it.

Not about him. About me.

Somewhere between the first after-hours coffee and the walks through quiet, unfamiliar streets… I had stepped out of the lines I had drawn for myself.

And I didn't regret it.

This wasn't love. Not yet.

But it wasn't nothing.

Because for the first time in years, I didn't feel like I was scripting the interaction, leading the experience, managing the tempo.

I was moving with someone.

And I wasn't in control.

That felt strange.

And real.

And dangerously right.

Chapter 16

The Rhythm

We didn't say it out loud. But a rhythm settled between us. Quietly. Without design.

Something had shifted. Not abruptly—but with the kind of certainty you only notice when it becomes part of your day.

Inside the office, we remained exactly who we were supposed to be.

I led. He executed.

We maintained the pace, the boundaries, the professionalism expected of us.

There were no delays in meetings. No casual eye contact during presentations. No change in tone when his name appeared on my schedule.

But underneath it all, I could feel the difference.

He didn't try to hold my attention. He didn't act entitled.

He moved through his tasks with the same quiet focus he always had—but there was something steadier in him now. A kind of knowing.

And in me, something gentler.

The others noticed too.

It began with harmless observations—his rise was quick, his access direct. People started paying closer attention to his presence. His growth was no longer just merit on paper—it became conversation.

Some framed it as timing. Others, as advantage.

I heard the murmurs. So did he.

But he never reacted. He never corrected them, never justified himself.

He kept showing up. Delivering. Listening more than he spoke.

And most importantly—he never changed with me.

Even when we were alone, he never acknowledged the talk. Never asked what I'd heard.

He left it outside the room, outside the hours, outside us.

That discipline—that stillness—earned him more than my respect. It kept our rhythm intact.

When I offered him the full-time position, I expected backlash.

And it came.

The questions weren't direct, but they were in the air.

"Was it performance or proximity?"

"Talent or timing?"

No one asked me. But I knew they were asking each other.

He knew too.

But if it hurt him, he didn't show it.

He didn't retreat. He didn't overcompensate.

He simply continued—with quiet conviction, like the noise around him didn't belong to him.

And that's when I knew: this wasn't something fragile.

It didn't need validation. It didn't seek definition.

It just was.

The best part?

He never let what we shared interfere with what we built separately.

He kept the day clean.

And whatever lived between us after hours—he never dragged it into boardrooms or blurred it into performance reviews.

There were evenings we didn't meet at all. Days when our only communication was a dry project brief.

And still, I never doubted the rhythm. Because it didn't need daily confirmation to be real.

It lived in silence. In consistency.

In how we navigated a world that watched us more than we spoke about each other.

This wasn't infatuation.

It didn't flare up. It didn't demand attention.

It just continued—like breath, like background music, like something designed to last.

We didn't overstay our evenings.

We didn't stretch conversations past their natural end.

We never let personal drift into public.

And that, I realized, was the foundation.

Not made of big gestures.

But small, quiet decisions that said:

We know what we're doing.

Even if we never said it out loud.

And then, one Friday evening, as I was closing my laptop, I saw a message from him:

"I want to show you something this weekend. Nothing professional. Just something you've never done. Hope you're free."

He didn't wait for a reply. Didn't explain. Didn't push. He just left it there. Simple. Direct.

I read it. Once. Twice. A third time. And for a moment, I didn't move.

The office was dim, the sun dipping low through the blinds. The hum of the AC was the only thing still working overtime.

My hands hovered over the keyboard, not because I didn't know what to say—but because this moment was rare.

This wasn't just an invitation. It was him opening a door, not into his world... but into a place he thought I might enjoy.

That alone meant everything.

I stood from my chair, walked to the window, and looked down at the city. The lights had started to flicker on—one floor at a time.

Behind me, my desk waited for a response. But inside me, something else stirred—something quiet, expectant.

I didn't rush to respond. Didn't overthink it.

But I smiled—the kind of smile that lives behind your eyes. The kind that doesn't need words.

Because for the first time in a very long time, I didn't feel like the woman who needed to lead every moment.

I just felt... ready.

It wasn't the kind of message that screams for attention. It was the kind that whispered to the part of me that had always been quiet.

Not a demand. Not an invitation for intimacy. Just a door.

And I was ready to open it.

Chapter 17

The Weekend He Designed

It was a Saturday. Crisp, clear, and quietly expectant.

He hadn't given much detail. Just a time. A location. And a line that felt more like a promise:

"No work shoes. No makeup. Just comfort. I'll bring the rest."

She arrived five minutes early. A narrow trail off a countryside road led her to a small, still lake—the kind most people drive past without noticing. Trees curled gently around the water's edge. Sunlight filtered through, soft and warm.

He was already there. A blanket laid out near the bank. A thermos. A paper bag. No stage. No flair.

Just presence.

When she stepped onto the blanket, she didn't say anything at first. She sat down. Crossed her legs. Looked at him.

"You planned all this?" she asked.

He shrugged with a smile. "As much as I could. The rest...I hoped would fall into place."

She looked around. No staff. No curated playlist. No

branded experience. Just the smell of earth. The sound of water brushing against the edge. And him.

"You know," she said, glancing at the thermos, "no one's ever done something this quiet for me."

He poured her coffee and handed it over without ceremony. "Figured you get enough noise Monday to Friday."

She took the cup. Took a sip. And watched him.

Not like a boss evaluating her team. Not like a woman trying to impress. But like someone seeing something… rare.

He opened the brown bag. "Sandwiches. Nothing fancy. I tried to guess what you'd like. There's peanut butter and apple in one. And tomato, mozzarella, and mint in the other."

She raised an eyebrow. "Peanut butter and apple?"

He smiled. "Thought you'd judge me. That's why I brought two."

She laughed. The kind of laugh she hadn't felt in years— loose, low, unguarded.

The breeze picked up slightly. Leaves rustled in approval. They ate slowly. No rush. No awkwardness.

She asked him how he found the spot. He said he used to bike around as a kid, finding quiet places to disappear into.

"I figured if you've built a world everyone wants a piece of… maybe it would feel good to sit in a world that wants nothing from you."

That stopped her.

She set her coffee down. Tucked a strand of hair behind her ear. And looked at him fully.

"You really thought all this through."

He shrugged again, casually. But she saw it now—the care beneath the calm. The intention behind every small thing.

She sat in front of him, folded knees and curious eyes, and just...looked. "I admire this," she said softly.

"This?" he asked.

"This. You. The effort. The quiet. The space you gave me today."

He didn't reply immediately. Just looked at her like someone who wasn't trying to win but simply *meant* it.

And in that stillness, something in her shifted again. Not with force. But with ease.

The lake rippled lightly in the background. And for the first time, she felt like she wasn't building anything.

She was just being. With him.

And it was enough. More than enough.

Suddenly, he stood up—without warning—and pulled a small speaker from his backpack. A soft jazz tune began to play, delicate and free. Then, right there on the grass, he started to dance.

She blinked, startled. "What are you doing?"

He spun once, laughed, and said, "Come on. Don't act so surprised."

She looked around, half-embarrassed, glancing toward a nearby couple sketching under a tree and a young girl strumming a guitar in the distance.

He caught her hesitation. "See? That's why I chose this place—no one judges anyone here."

He pointed toward the trees. "Look at them—they learn music without fear. Look at the artist—he draws what he admires, not what sells."

Then he turned back to her. "Likewise, I just happen to like dancing on picnics. It's my thing."

He reached out a hand, still moving lightly to the rhythm. "One step. Try it. Giving it a try never harmed anyone."

She hesitated—then exhaled. Slowly, she rose to her feet. She took his hand and stepped once into the music. Then again. Then again.

And to her surprise, it didn't feel awkward. It didn't feel watched. It felt like breathing.

She laughed—the kind of laugh that brings tears to the edges of your eyes. She let herself move, not to impress, not to perform—but to feel.

They danced. The song ended.

And the sunset arrived quietly, like a curtain drawing itself.

Their chatter softened. They lay on the blanket in silence for a while.

When they finally stood to leave, the artist—the one who had been sketching quietly all day—approached them with a small board wrapped in craft paper.

"My lady," he said with a bow, "this is my present to you. I've never seen such an honestly joyful woman before. It felt like a poem to me. I hope you like it."

She took the wrapped canvas with a stunned smile, peeled back the edges, and gasped.

It was her. Laughing. Mid-step. Caught in motion, captured without vanity.

She clutched the sketch to her chest. "Thank you," she whispered.

The artist nodded and walked away, humming the same jazz tune they had danced to.

She turned to him—the man of her choice. They walked back to the car. She didn't say much. She didn't need to.

But in her silence, something glowed. It was joy.

And maybe—just maybe—the beginning of something more.

Chapter 18

A Heart Full

She walked into her room with a mood she hadn't felt in years—maybe ever. Light. Joyful. Full.

She closed the door behind her with unusual gentleness. No rush. No weight. Just a kind of reverence—as if the air itself had shifted around her. She wasn't walking into her room. She was walking into a feeling.

She sat on the edge of her bed, pulled her heels off one by one, and let her body collapse back onto the mattress. The ceiling fan moved slowly overhead. The walls were quiet. But inside her? Everything pulsed.

She thought of him.

And then—a thought came, soft and sudden:

"Wow. The woman I am now… I feel like a baby. I laugh without filters. I look forward to mornings. I notice small things—like the way his sleeve rolls up when he pours coffee, or the pause before he smiles. It's new. It's innocent. It's pure."

She blinked. Sat up slowly. Her heart wasn't racing—it was humming.

"Maybe this…this feeling—this is what I was always waiting for."

It wasn't about perfection anymore. It wasn't about

control or power or building the ideal image.

It was about **presence**. It was about feeling like herself—not the empire, not the brand—but the *woman beneath all that*. The one who still hoped, quietly, that love could be something gentle and true.

"It took me 21 years to feel this. Maybe... maybe this is the universe's way of showing me—the man I was waiting for... is the one I created."

She stood and walked over to the mirror.

There she was. Sharp. Clear. Still her. But now with softness in her gaze. A kind of awe.

"Do I ever tell him the truth? That he was shaped—built—for this moment?" She paused.

"No. I shouldn't. Not now. That's not how this story will unfold. I'll handle that...in my way."

She turned away from the mirror and walked to her writing desk. Pushed away the stack of papers. Ignored the blinking email notifications. Closed the planner. Flipped the phone screen down.

No business meetings. No strategic calls. No global updates. Only one thought lived in her mind.

"Right now, the only thought in my mind...is him."

She chuckled—the kind of laugh that's half-surprise, half-relief.

"This isn't me. This...this emotional spiral—it's not how I operate. But maybe...this is the me I've been designing all these years. The one who feels deeply. The one who lives the love, not just imagines

it.“

She walked to the window.

The city lights blinked beneath her.

So much noise. So much structure. Yet here she stood— feeling weightless.

"I don't know how to explain this to anyone. I don't know whom to call and say, 'The man of my choice… he's real. And I think… I love him."

She stood still for a while. Let the silence stretch. And then suddenly, she turned.

"Before it gets too late. I should propose."

Her fingers hovered in the air like she was reaching for something invisible.

"Wait. Shouldn't he be the one to propose? Shouldn't I wait?"

She paced, her arms folding then unfolding, her breath light but unsettled.

"But what if he takes his time? What if I spend nights like this— tangled in thought, sipping cold coffee, dreaming instead of living?"

She exhaled long and slow.

"Okay… Patience is a virtue, right?"

A small grin crept to her lips. She sat down, pulled her legs up to the couch, and hugged a pillow to her chest.

She closed her eyes.

And in the darkness behind her lids, the memories bloomed:

·   His charismatic presence the day they first spoke.

·   That effortless smile that softened even her toughest moments.

·   The way his voice steadied her without needing to try.

·   That dance—silly, bold, free—and the laughter that followed.

·   His professional restraint, the way he carried himself like he belonged.

·   The compliments he gave her—not grand, but true. Rare. Specific. Each memory came with a scent, a sound, and a pause.

She felt every one of them—like a song she hadn't realised was her favourite until it played on repeat.

She opened her eyes slowly. Her heart wasn't pounding. It was preparing.

"This is more than enough. This is what I've waited for."

She reached for her phone. Opened a new message. Typed slowly, deliberately.

"Meet me tomorrow. Same place we had our first meeting. I have something to say."

She reread it. Then again. Then hit send.

She placed the phone down. Pressed her palms to her chest. And whispered to the empty room:

"Let that place become ours—from professional to personal."

She didn't sleep early that night. She changed outfits three times before laughing at herself. She poured tea, then forgot it. Picked up a book, then set it down.

She stayed up, tossing in bed, smiling into the dark. Not anxious. Just... alive.

Excited. Tense. Hopeful.

Because tomorrow... might be the moment everything aligns. Or changes.

Forever.

Chapter 19

The Proposal (Part 1)

The day began like a gentle hum beneath her skin. But unlike any other morning, it wasn't her calendar that dictated her rhythm—it was the anticipation of six o'clock.

She chose her dress with the care of a curator, not just for beauty, but for energy. Deep emerald silk—calm, composed, alluring. Hair tied with intention. Skin glowing like aged wine under soft light. Her aura? Not boss. Not an icon. Just a woman.

She had handled mergers, crises, and global collaborations with a single email and no pulse spike. But today? She felt something she hadn't in years: nervousness. It didn't paralyse her. It awakened something—something gentle, youthful, and almost sacred.

The meetings were quietly rescheduled. Her staff noticed her lightness, a rare softness that appeared only when something mattered beyond the boardroom. They didn't know what had shifted. But she did.

By 5:45, she had stopped pretending to be immersed in work. Her eyes flicked to the clock every few minutes. It felt like she was waiting for a train—one she had designed

21 years ago, and that was finally arriving on schedule.

When the hands hit 6:00, she stood. Confident. Composed. But with a quiet heartbeat fluttering under the surface.

She passed his desk. Empty.

Her brows twitched—not in worry, but in instinct.

Maybe he left early. Maybe he's already there.

The car ride was quiet. Not even music. Her thoughts were louder than melodies. She wasn't planning what to say. She didn't want to. This wasn't a pitch. This was presence.

When she arrived, the air kissed her with a soft evening breeze. She looked around. The chair they always chose. Empty. The terrace corner. Empty.

She stood for a moment, letting the light warm her skin. And then—

A silhouette emerged from the end of the path. The kind of presence that draws attention without asking for it.

Cuffs folded. Shirt pristine. Hair perfectly undone. Laptop tucked neatly. He walked like someone who didn't know the world was watching, but the world was watching anyway.

He looked like a man who didn't belong to a company. He looked like a man who belonged to himself.

Every woman in that café turned.

But he didn't notice them.

He noticed her.

And when he approached, a mischievous spark glimmered in his eyes.

"Добрый вечер" (Dobryy vecher), he said with a grin.

She paused, caught off guard for half a second, then smiled. "Добрый вечер" (Dobryy vecher), she returned.

He laughed. "You speak Russian too?"

She tilted her head with mock surprise. "You didn't know we have a flagship branch in Moscow?"

"Point taken. But...wait—are we talking business now?"

"Only to prove I'm smarter than you," she winked.

He chuckled, pulling out the chair across from her. "Okay, fair. So, what's this about?"

She exhaled through a gentle smile. "I have something to say. Something important."

Just then, as if on cue, the waiter approached.

"Mam, your regular order?"

She shot him a glance. "Yes. And don't announce it next time."

The waiter turned to him. "And for you, sir?"

He named his favourite—a dish she hadn't heard of. She noted that. She always remembered what mattered.

The table settled. The air between them grew charged, but not tense.

She leaned in slightly. "It's been a month. And in that

month... we've talked. Laughed. Met without expectations. And I—"

He leaned in too. "You...?"

Her breath came slow. "I just wanted to be honest about something I haven't shared."

He didn't speak. Just nodded, inviting.

And in that silence, something beautiful happened.

She didn't rush. She didn't prepare a speech. She didn't even know if she'd say it all today.

But she knew this: she wasn't afraid. Not of rejection. Not of exposure. Because for the first time in her life, she wasn't proving. She was just being.

She watched him. He was listening—not to reply, but to understand.

She looked down for a second, then up again. "I think I've come to value something far beyond control or success."

He smiled gently.

"And that is?"

She paused. Not for drama. For clarity.

"Connection that doesn't need to be managed."

The words hovered. Not quite a confession. But something close.

He nodded slowly, digesting that. The waiter returned briefly with their drinks, interrupting the moment just enough to breathe.

She wrapped her fingers around the glass but didn't sip. Her eyes never left his face.

And in that quiet space of clinking glasses and quiet chatter around them, something shifted.

They were no longer a boss and an employee. They were two souls standing in a field of unspoken possibility.

And the night had just begun.

Chapter 20

The Proposal (Part 2)

The café lights seemed to blur, like watercolour in motion. Outside, the streetlamps hummed. Inside, time folded inward.

She had just said it. There was no hesitation. No uncertainty. No second-guessing dressed as humility.

She looked him in the eye and said,

"I've fallen for you."

He looked at her. Not through her. Not around her. But *at her.*

And something in his breath shifted. A pause. A weight.

He had always been calm. He handled chaos like a composed flame—never out of control, always just enough.

But now? Even his pulse betrayed him.

He blinked. Took it in her face. The one he'd seen every day for months—powerful, poised... and now, open.

She waited. Not like a girl hoping. But like a woman *knowing* this mattered.

The silence stretched. It wasn't awkward. It was *loud.*

Finally, he exhaled—not relief, not regret—just confusion woven into compassion.

"I don't know how to say no… because I don't want to hurt you."

She didn't flinch. She looked him in the eye.

"Why?" she asked. Her voice was soft and steady. "Is it my age?"

"No." He shook his head quickly. "It's not your age. Not your beauty. Not anything you might blame."

"Then what?" she asked. Not angry. Just… needing.

He leaned forward. "It's us."

She tilted her head. "Us?"

"You see me as the man of your choice," he said, gently.

"I do."

"I fit your expectations. A hundred percent?"

"Yes."

He paused. Looked down. His fingers traced the edge of his glass. Then he met her eyes again.

"Did you ever stop to think…"

She raised a hand. "Wait. I can't hold it anymore. Just say it."

And he did.

"As I fill your expectations… you don't fill mine."

The café disappeared in that moment.

Not in sound. But in feeling.

It was like someone turned the world on mute. Her breath. Her heart. Her mind—all slowed.

She felt everything… all at once. Twenty-one years of strategy. Of planning. Of dreaming.

All collapsing into a single truth she never calculated: *He doesn't feel the same.*

She thought of the journals, the candles, and the carefully curated life she built for his arrival. She thought of the silence she preserved, the emotions she avoided, and the love she postponed—just to meet him cleanly.

And still, she wasn't the one.

Her chest didn't ache. It caved.

Not because he rejected her. But because for the first time, she realised:

This wasn't a heartbreak. This was the end of her illusion.

And in a whisper not meant for him, but for the ache inside her, she said—

"Oh."

He tried to soften it. "You're extraordinary. You're brilliant. You're the most present human I've ever met."

"But you don't love me."

He didn't answer. That *was* the answer.

And slowly, the realisation unwrapped itself inside her.

She hadn't just created a man. She had created a future.

A timeline. A belief.

She had convinced herself that building the perfect structure would guarantee the perfect bond.

But this was the truth she never anticipated:

Even your masterpiece can walk away.

She blinked once. Twice. Not to hold back tears—but to stay present.

It wasn't betrayal. It wasn't disappointment. It was simply this—

He didn't choose her.

And for the first time in her life, she realised:

Control can build empires. But it can't build love.

She stood. Not because she wanted to leave, but because she couldn't sit in the hollow any longer.

She looked down at him, the man of her design—and smiled. A real one. The kind that breaks you as it heals.

"Thank you," she said. "For being honest."

He nodded. Didn't try to stop her. Didn't explain.

Because this wasn't a story of right and wrong. It was a story of one-sided readiness.

And as she walked away, her heels echoing softly into the night, she thought—

She had waited twenty-one years. And in those years, she became everything. To the world. To herself.

But she couldn't become what he felt.

She had *found* the man of her choice. But she wasn't the woman of his.

And that... That was the truth her empire could never shield her from.

She didn't cry. She didn't shatter.

But something inside her exhaled.

And in that exhale, the reader will know—

She didn't lose. She learnt.

And what she learnt will stay.

Forever.

SHE:

I spent years designing a man who would match me in every way.

His mind. His rhythm. His presence.

I removed the noise. The ego. The chaos.

And in the end, I met him—

A man who *should* have been everything.

But love doesn't arrive just because you planned it.

I learnt something the hard way:

There is no such thing as a "100% match" before love begins.

You can align values. Curate energy. Shape ideals.

But love?

It's not in the design.

It's in the connection.

Don't wait for someone to tick every box.

Don't hold a measuring scale in your hand.

If someone gives you even a part of what you hoped for,

and you feel something real—honest, steady, kind. —

Start there.

Because love doesn't come *after* perfection.

Love is what makes it whole.

Not 100% on paper.

100% in feeling.

And if it doesn't come—even after everything?

That's not failure.

That's clarity.

Because you can build a masterpiece…

But even a masterpiece deserves to be chosen back.

www.ingramcontent.com/pod-product-compliance
Lightning Source LLC
Chambersburg PA
CBHW052013240626
47153CB00008B/2864